Mail Carriers

Risa Brown

FITZGERALD
BOOKS

Bethany, Missouri

Photo Credits:
Cover © Steve Snyder, P.I.R.; Title Page © Tomasz Szymanski; Page 4 © Bunny Lady; Page 5 © Dan Blais; Page 7, 8, 11, 12, 21 © Canada Post Corporation; Page 9 © Steve Snyder; Page 13 © Linda Armstrong; Page 15 © Lisa Eastman; Page 17 © Michelle Malven; Page 19 © Sean Locke; Page 20 © Scott A. Frangos, Slobo; Page 22 © Jane M. Sawyer

Cataloging-in-Publication Data

Brown, Risa W.
    Mail carriers / Risa Brown. — 1st ed.
    p. cm. — (Community helpers)

    Includes bibliographical references and index.
    Summary: Text and photographs introduce mail carriers,
from the service they provide and the mail they handle, to their
daily work routines, uniforms, and more.
    ISBN-13: 978-1-4242-1355-9 (lib. bdg. : alk. paper)
    ISBN-10: 1-4242-1355-X (lib. bdg. : alk. paper)
    ISBN-13: 978-1-4242-1445-7 (pbk. : alk. paper)
    ISBN-10: 1-4242-1445-9 (pbk. : alk. paper)

    1. Letter carriers—United States—Juvenile literature.
2. Postal service—Vocational guidance—Juvenile literature.
[1. Letter carriers. 2. Postal service—Employees. 3. Postal service—
Vocational guidance.
4. Occupations.] I. Brown, Risa W. II. Title. III. Series.
    HE6499.B76 2007
    383'.145—dc22

First edition
© 2007 Fitzgerald Books
802 N. 41st Street, P.O. Box 505
Bethany, MO 64424, U.S.A.
Printed in China
Library of Congress Control Number: 2007900208

Table of Contents

Mail at Your House

Mail carriers make sure you get your mail. They pick up mail you want to send.

5

Early Morning

Mail carriers start their days early, sorting the mail at the **post office**. They make sure the right mail gets to the right house.

Into the Truck

Mail carriers load the mail into their trucks. Mail trucks have steering wheels on the "wrong" side so they can be driven up close to **mailboxes**.

9

Stops

Most mail carriers walk the same **routes** every day. They bring the mail to homes, offices, and businesses. They pick up mail that needs to be sent.

Busy, Busy, Busy

Mail carriers work hard. They lift heavy boxes and carry full **pouches**.

They climb in and out of their trucks and walk a long way.

Hazards

Mail carriers have to be careful. Rain, ice, or snow could make sidewalks and streets slick. Mean dogs sometimes bite.

Uniforms

Mail carriers' **uniforms** match the time of year. They wear warm clothes in winter and shorts in the summer.

Important Mail

Sometimes mail carriers need people to sign when they deliver special mail. If the person is not home, mail carriers leave a note on the door.

Out and About

Some mail carriers pick up mail from large mailboxes called bins.

All mail carriers can answer any mail-related question.

Back to the Post Office

Mail carriers return to the post office with the mail they picked up. Your mail is sent to wherever you need it to go.

Glossary

mail carrier (MAL KAR e er) — a person who delivers the mail

mailbox (MAL bocks) — a box nearby or on a house where mail is delivered

post office (POST OFF iss) — a place where mail is sorted and stamps are sold

pouch (POUCH) — a bag to carry mail

route (ROUT) — a regular path a mail carrier follows each day

uniform (YU ne form) — clothes that are the same for all postal workers

Index

FURTHER READING

Klingel, Cynthia and Robert B. Noved. *Postal Workers*. Child's World, 2002.
Macken, JoAnne Early. *Mail Carrier*. Weekly Reader, 2003.
Trumbauer, Lisa. *What Does a Mail Carrier Do?* Enslow, 2005.

WEBSITES TO VISIT

Because Internet links change so often, Fitzgerald Books has developed an online list of websites related to the subject of this book. This site is updated regularly. Please use this link to access the list: www.fitzgeraldbookslinks.com/ch/mc

ABOUT THE AUTHOR

Risa Brown was a librarian for twenty years before becoming a full-time writer. Now living in Dallas, she grew up in Midland, Texas, President George W. Bush's hometown.